The Crook that Made Kids CRY

by
Steve Brezenoff

illustrated by
Marcos Calo

STONE ARCH BOOKS
a capstone imprint

f Samantha Archer,

Field Trip Mysteries are published by Stone Arch Books
A Capstone Imprint
1710 Roe Crest Drive
North Mankato, Minnesota 55603
www.capstonepub.com

Library of Congress Cataloging-in-Publication Data
Brezenoff, Steven.
    The crook that made kids cry / by Steve Brezenoff ;
illustrated by Marcos Calo.
       p. cm. -- (Field trip mysteries)
    ISBN 978-1-4342-5977-6 (library binding)
    ISBN 978-1-4342-6210-3 (pbk.)
1. School field trips--Juvenile fiction. 2. Children's museums-
-Juvenile fiction. 3. Vandalism--Juvenile fiction. [1. Mystery
and detective stories. 2. School field trips--Fiction. 3.
Children's museums--Fiction. 4. Museums--Fiction. 5. Vandalism-
-Fiction.] I. Calo, Marcos, ill. II. Title. III. Series:
Brezenoff, Steven. Field trip mysteries.
    PZ7.B7576Cqt 2013   2012049375
    813.6--dc23

Graphic Designer: Kristi Carlson

Summary: Sam Archer, her friends, and their
"kindergarten buddies" are on a trip to a
children's museum, which has been plagued by
vandalism.

Printed in China.
032013   007228RRDF13

TABLE OF CONTENTS

Samantha Archer

A.K.A: Sam

D.O.B: August 20th

POSITION: 6th Grade

Why are these kids so interested in field trips? I will look into this!

INTERESTS:

Old movies, field trips

KNOWN ASSOCIATES:

Duran, Catalina; Garrison, Edward; and Shoo, James.

NOTES:

Samantha frequently uses expressions many of the students—and even some of the teachers—do not understand. These seem to come from the old movies she watches at home.

Samantha recently called me Mr. Spade's "Bruno." What does this mean? I will look into this, too.

KINDERGARTEN BUDDIES

The last thing I wanted to do was join Kindergarten Buddies.

Kindergarten Buddies is this program that sets up sixth graders with kindergartners for special events and activities.

I'm not a little kid person. But sometimes, when your friends are doing something, and when your grandparents — the same grandparents who raised you your whole life — encourage you very strongly to join your friends, you don't really have a choice.

So I joined. I trudged through the snow one Monday morning in February. It was some president's birthday, and every normal kid in River City had the day off.

But not the Kindergarten Buddies. We were stuck going to the children's museum for the day. This would be the lamest field trip in Franklin Middle School history. And I'd be stuck with a little kid named . . .

"Samuel Needleman," said Teacher Todd. Teacher Todd is in charge of the Kindergarten Buddies program. He talks to everyone, including the sixth graders, like they're little kids.

A little boy with jet-black hair stepped out of the little gang of kindergartners. His face was thick with dark freckles.

He put out his hand like a big shot. "Hello," he said. "Most people call me Sam."

I glared at Teacher Todd. "You gave me a kid named Sam?" I said. "*My* name is Sam." It's Samantha Archer, but everyone calls me Sam.

Teacher Todd giggled. "I know!" he said. "I knew you'd think it was fun!"

Fun? Hardly. He moved on, though, to Cat — that's Catalina Duran, my best friend.

"Cat," Teacher Todd said, "this is Penelope Hornwhistle." He grinned ear to ear. "She loves animals as much as you do. And she has a special name today."

Up stepped a girl with curly, black hair pulled back in a short ponytail. She went right to Cat. "Hi!" she said. "My new nickname will be Puppy, because you're Cat!"

She talked like everything was the most exciting thing of all time. I rolled my eyes.

Cat ate it up, though. She flashed a smile, and I swear I thought she would cry from joy. She grabbed the little girl's hands, and they both jumped up and down shouting, "Cat and Puppy! Cat and Puppy!"

I nearly cried myself, but not from joy.

"And next," Teacher Todd said, "we have Edward Garrison's buddy."

Edward is another of my best friends. We usually call him Egg.

"Edward, this is Chloe Carmichael," Teacher Todd said. He waved toward a tall girl with blonde hair and glasses.

With her eyes on her feet, Chloe stepped around the group. "Hello," she said quietly. Egg went over to her, and I nearly laughed. They were almost the same height!

Egg smiled at her. "Nice to meet you," he said. Then he raised his camera — it's always hanging around his neck — and snapped her picture.

I think the flash nearly blinded her. She flinched and covered her eyes.

"Oops, sorry," Egg said. "I didn't mean to startle you. I love taking pictures. I take pictures of everything."

Then Chloe looked at him, smiling like crazy. She quickly turned to Teacher Todd. "Can I go to my cubby?" she asked. He nodded, and she hurried off. A moment later she ran back.

You'll never guess what she was carrying.

"This is *my* camera!" she said, holding it out to Egg. It was basically a smaller version of Egg's camera.

Egg's eyes went wide behind his glasses. He grabbed the camera from her and looked it over. He peered through the viewfinder. Then he handed it back to her. "That is a great camera you got there," he said.

"Thanks," she said. All her shyness was gone now. "I got it for my birthday. I just turned six. You can take a few pictures with it if you want to."

Then she took a picture of Egg. They were obviously best friends already, just like Cat and Penelope. Oh, sorry. I mean Puppy.

Teacher Todd had a few more Buddies to introduce, including Gum's buddy. Gum is my other best friend. His real name is James Shoo, but we've called him Gum since the very first field trip mystery we solved.

Teacher Todd called for a little boy named Connor Linden. I figured he'd have the nickname "Candy" or something. But I didn't have a chance to find out, because just then the door of the little classroom banged open.

"Hello, dorks," said Anton Gutman as he stomped in.

If Gum, Cat, and Egg are my best friends, then Anton is my worst enemy. He's in our class, so he's always on field trips with us.

But none of us expected to see him on a Kindergarten Buddies trip.

"What are you doing here, Anton?" Gum asked. He likes Anton least of all of us. Gum always thinks Anton is the criminal in one of our mysteries.

Anton ignored Gum and walked right over to a boy standing with Teacher Todd. "Hey, Skip," Anton said. The little boy had hair just like Anton's and a sneer just like Anton's.

Oh, no, I thought. *It can't be.*

I glanced at Gum. He glanced at me. We both glanced at Egg and Cat. The looks on their face betrayed their panic. It was true. There was no other explanation.

"Of course," Teacher Todd said. "The perfect buddy for Anton Gutman: his little brother, Skip!"

AT THE MUSEUM

"I can't believe there are two Gutmans,"
said Egg. The four of us — actually, the eight
of us, including our Buddies — sat in the back
of the van. We were on our way to the River
City Children's Museum for a field trip.

Teacher Todd was driving. At the front of
the van, sitting right behind him, were Anton
and Skip Gutman. They were both turned
around in the seat, sneering back toward us.

"I don't like that boy Skip," said Cat's new
buddy, Puppy. "He pulls my hair."

"His brother isn't very nice either," Cat said.

Egg snapped a picture of the Gutmans. The flash alerted Teacher Todd. He looked in the rearview mirror and, smiling, told Anton and Skip to face forward. They did.

"So, Connor," Gum asked. "What are you most excited to do at the museum?"

"Water World?" Cat suggested.

"The Shadow Screen?" Egg asked.

Connor shook his head. He didn't smile. His mouth was set and hard, like a real tough guy. I thought maybe I'd like this kid.

"I'm just looking forward to catching Skip in the act," he said. "He always picks on someone on field trips. And he always breaks loads of rules. Today, I'm going to catch him."

"Just like his brother," Gum said. "You and I have a lot in common. I think we'll get along great."

So Gum and Connor both hated the Gutman boys. Cat and her buddy both loved animals. And Egg and Chloe loved taking pictures. Maybe Little Sam and I had something in common too.

"Okay, buddy," I said. "What do you like at the museum? The Clues Room? The Movie Studio? Anything like that?"

"Well," he said, "my favorite thing at the museum is the Book Nook."

"The Book Nook?" I said. "Oh, is that like where storybooks come to life or something?"

"Nope," he said. "It's a little seating area on the third floor with books. It's usually pretty quiet. Most kids don't go there."

"That sounds . . . " I started to say. But I stopped myself. The only word I could think of to finish that sentence was "boring."

The van bumped to a stop at the curb in front of the museum. We all piled off.

Teacher Todd got off last. He stood in front of the museum's glass doors.

"Everyone," he said, "please hold hands with your buddy whenever we're on the move. That means . . ."

"When we're not playing!" all the kindergartners called out. Well, almost all of them. I noticed Skip Gutman didn't say anything. He just mouthed along with the others with a nasty look on his face.

After we got all checked in, Teacher Todd led us into the Big Room. A bunch of chairs were set up, all facing the same direction.

"Everyone, please sit down with your buddy," said Teacher Todd.

Just then, a man walked in. He wore a suit with the museum's logo on the lapel. "Hello, Kindergarten Buddies!" he said. "We are so glad to have you with us at the museum today. I'm the museum's director, Mr. Bundt."

"Hello, Mr. Bundt!" the kindergartners said. This time, we were ready, so the sixth graders joined in too.

The Gutmans didn't, though. They just snickered. I'm sure they thought the man's name was funny or something.

"We'll get you kids off for a fun day in a few moments," said Mr. Bundt, "but first, I'll run through some of the museum rules."

There weren't many rules, and they were kind of silly ones. One was, "Do not touch any items in the museum, with the following exceptions: everything on the first, second, and third floors." There were only three floors, so that meant you could touch anything.

There was also, "Everyone must walk in a single file, except when they do not," and, "Grown-ups must be with a child."

Finally, Mr. Bundt said, "Okay, everyone have fun. That's the most important rule." Then his phone rang. "Excuse me," he said.

He pulled the phone out of his pocket as he headed for the door. I could tell from the look on his face as he checked the incoming call that he wasn't happy about it.

Teacher Todd led us out of the room. "Everyone is free to explore the museum," he said. "Just be sure to stay with your buddy."

I knelt down and did my best to smile at Little Sam. "So what do you want to do first?"

"Book Nook, please," he said. At least he was polite. "We can take the elevator."

"Okay," I said. I waved good-bye to my friends. They headed off with their Buddies to the Water World, the Work Zone, and the Shadow Screen. Any of those would have been more fun than the boring old Book Nook.

The elevators seemed to take forever. Little Sam stood next to me, holding my hand, staring at the glowing "up" button. Finally the bell dinged, the doors opened, and we stepped onto the third floor.

It was quiet. The only things on the floor were the Book Nook and a room for babies and toddlers. Hanging from the ceiling, over the stairwell, were some big bird sculptures.

Little Sam plodded over to the little couch and grabbed a book. It was an easy-reader, and there were lots of pictures. Still, for a kindergartner, he was advanced.

He opened the book and then put it back right away. I sat down next to him as he grabbed another. He opened that one too, and then put it back right away.

"Aren't you going to read them?" I said.

"I can't," he said.

"Oh," I said. I guessed I was wrong about him being advanced. "Should I read to you?"

He rolled his eyes. "I know *how* to read," he said. "I mean, I can't read these." He handed one to me. "See? They're all like this."

I opened the book.
Every page had been
ripped out.

CHAPTER THREE

PRIME SUSPECTS

Little Sam wasn't happy. I tried to cheer him up, telling him all about the fun things we could do at the other exhibits.

"There's one where you can control a crane truck!" I said. "Doesn't every little boy love crane trucks?"

"I like them okay," he said glumly. "But I'd rather read the book about trucks up in the Book Nook."

"Right," I said.

We found Gum and Connor at the Work Zone. Connor was struggling to push a cart full of fake bricks and pipes.

Gum was wearing an orange worker's vest. It was way too small on him. He was sure a good sport.

"Having fun?" Gum asked as we walked up.

"Not really," I said. I looked down at Little Sam. "Right, kid?"

He nodded. "Some vandal destroyed all the books in the Book Nook," he explained to Gum. "It was probably Skip Gutman. He does stuff like that all the time."

Gum and Connor froze in place. Connor stopped pushing his cart and turned to look at me and Little Sam.

"This is it," said Connor. He walked over to join us. Gum put a hand on his shoulder.

"It's the chance I've been waiting for," Connor said, looking up at his buddy.

"I know, Connor," said Gum, nodding. "I know. Me too."

"What in the world are you talking about?" I asked. Little Sam chuckled, I think.

"We're talking about catching Skip Gutman in the act," Connor said.

"But the act is over," I pointed out. "There's no evidence. Just Little Sam's hunch."

"We'll see about that," said Gum. I had to give him credit: he was a sharp investigator. Maybe he'd find something.

"Besides," said Connor, "this cart is busted."

"What's wrong with it?" asked Little Sam.

Connor pointed at its wheels.

"See for yourself," he said. He took Gum by the hand, and off they went.

Little Sam and I walked over to the full cart. I got down on one knee and Little Sam leaned over. One of the wheels was missing.

"Another vandal attack," Little Sam said as we stood up. "I guess the Gutmans have been busy today."

"I suppose they are the prime suspects so far," I admitted, "but we don't have any hard evidence."

"They're both meanies," Little Sam said.

I laughed. "I don't think that would hold up in court," I said.

"I guess not," he replied.

I reached for his hand. "Come on," I said. "Let's find the photographers."

We found Egg and Chloe in the baby room on the third floor. I didn't even think we should check there, but Little Sam had a hunch.

"Chloe really likes babies," he said. "I bet she's there, taking pictures."

And sure enough, she was. Egg looked bored out of his mind. I guess babies weren't his favorite photography subject.

"You two having any fun?" I asked Egg.

Little Sam found a place to sit down near the window. There was a picture book there, so he started reading.

"We were," Egg said. "Chloe was posing for the Shadow Screen."

That's this crazy exhibit where your shadows freeze on the wall behind you, even after you start moving again.

"I took some cool pictures," Egg said. He held out the display on his camera and flipped through. They were pretty cool. Chloe's shadow didn't match up with her pose at all.

"So why'd you come up here?" I asked.

"That's the weird thing," Egg said. "There was a funny smell, and then the screen just stopped working."

"Really?" I said. "Sounds like maybe our vandals are back." I told him what had happened in the Book Nook and the Work Zone.

"Do you think it's the Gutmans?" Egg asked.

"They're our top suspects, but the evidence is pretty thin," I said.

Little Sam grabbed my hand. "I need to use the bathroom," he said.

"That's my cue," I said to Egg. "See you later."

Little Sam and I headed for the door to leave the baby room. As we did, though, a mom shrieked.

"What is that?" she yelled. "There's a big puddle over here!"

"It's probably pee!" someone else shouted.

I looked at Sam. "It wasn't me!" he said.

We hurried back in to check it out. The moms were all standing around, holding their babies against their chests, as if the pee were a toxic chemical spill.

Egg and Chloe snapped like a hundred photos apiece.

"What happened?" I asked Egg. He shrugged.

The moms had seen enough. They all grabbed their bags and babies and strollers and headed for the door.

"The weird thing," I said, "is that it doesn't smell like pee." I knelt next to the big puddle. It nearly filled the whole plush garden section of the baby area.

I sniffed it. "Nope, not pee," I said. "I think it's . . . apple juice?"

After a stop at the bathroom, Egg, Chloe, Little Sam, and I took the steps down to the first floor.

It was nearly time for our lunch break. We were meeting in the lobby. Then we would walk to the food court in the mall, which was connected to the museum.

"Who would pour apple juice on the floor?" Egg asked.

"In a room full of babies?" I said. "Anyone might have spilled some apple juice."

"I guess," said Egg. "But with all the other stuff that's happened — the missing wheel, the ripped-up books, the broken Shadow Screen — I figure someone's going to a lot of trouble to get people out of the museum."

"It does seem that way," I said. "I guess we have a vandal on our hands."

Gum, Cat, and their Buddies were already in the lobby. Then the Gutman boys showed up, snickering and pushing each other. They were obviously up to something. But Teacher Todd was calling for our attention, so we'd have to investigate later.

"We are heading into the mall," Teacher Todd said. "It will be busy and crowded, so stick with your Buddies. Now, off to the food court!"

* * *

At the food court, our group stopped to survey what our options were. There were burgers, tacos, salads, smoothies, and pizza. Of course, everyone wanted something different.

Luckily, Little Sam and I both wanted tacos. We headed toward Taco Time and got in line.

"Hey, it's Mr. Bundt," said Little Sam. He pointed at the front of the line. There was the children's museum director, ordering his food.

"I'll have three spicy tacos and —" His phone rang, interrupting him. He pulled it out of his pocket and turned away from the cashier.

"Hello?" he said. "I can't talk right now. . . . I've already told you. . . . Tell your boss the museum isn't going anywhere!"

Finally Mr. Bundt put his cell phone away and finished ordering. Soon it was our turn.

"I'm having ten tacos!" Little Sam shouted as we reached the register.

"Um, I don't think so," I said, smiling at the cashier. She wasn't amused. "We'll have one taco for the little guy, and I'll have a burrito."

"Aww," said Little Sam. "I wanted ten."

Little Sam insisted on carrying our tray, so it took forever to walk to the table where my friends were sitting. I was anxious to tell them what we'd overheard Mr. Bundt saying on the phone. It might have nothing to do with the vandalism, but when you're on a case, you have to notice every little thing.

"Come on, Sam," I said. "Our food is getting cold. I can carry the tray."

"I can do it!" he said, gripping the tray. He shuffled along with tiny, careful steps, his eyes on the taco the whole time.

I was losing patience. Finally I couldn't take it anymore. "Look, I'm going to walk ahead and tell my friends something," I said.

"Okay," Little Sam said. He still didn't take his eyes off that taco.

"See where we're sitting?" I said. I pointed ahead of us to where our group was sitting. "I'm going right there, okay?"

"Okay!" he said. But he still didn't look up.

I mussed his hair a second. Then I jogged over to the table and sat down. "So," I said, "guess who I just overheard on his phone?"

"Anton Gutman?" Gum asked.

"Skip Gutman?" Connor said.

"Nope," I said. "Mr. Bundt, the museum director."

"So?" said Egg. "He's not a suspect, is he? Why would he vandalize his own museum?"

"It sounds like someone wants to get rid of the museum," I explained. "Mr. Bundt was angry about it."

"Who would want to get rid of the museum?" Cat asked.

"What a terrible thing to do!" Puppy said. She and Cat smiled at each other.

"Aren't you eating anything?" Gum asked me as he took a big bite of his hamburger.

"Oh, yeah," I said. "A burrito. Little Sam is —" I looked up. "He should have been here by now."

I stood up and looked all around. He was nowhere in sight.

Little Sam was
gone.

"I can't believe you lost your buddy," Gum said. He shook his head.

"Be quiet and help me find him!" I said. We'd dumped our lunches and were frantically searching the food court.

"We have to tell Teacher Todd," Cat said. "He's over there, by the yogurt stand."

"Wait!" I said, grabbing her wrist. "I'll get in so much trouble."

Cat put her hands on her hips. She frowned at me.

"Please," I said. "Five minutes."

She sighed. "I can't, Sam," she said. "If something happened to Little Sam, every second could be important."

With Puppy's hand in hers, Cat jogged off toward Teacher Todd. From where I stood, I could see as she stopped next to his chair. It looked like she interrupted a conversation he was having with a man I didn't recognize.

Teacher Todd's mouth opened, and he got to his feet. His head spun like ten times as he looked for Little Sam.

He put his hands to his mouth like a megaphone. "Sam!" he shouted. "Samuel!"

I took a deep breath. Then I started walking toward Teacher Todd to take my lecture. But I didn't make it.

Just a few steps later, I passed a row of trash cans. Squatting behind them was a little boy with tears on his cheeks.

"Sam!" I said. "Are you okay? What happened? Where did you go?"

"I was walking," he said, crying. "And I got to your table. But when I looked up, I was at the wrong table."

"Oh," I said. "You couldn't find us?"

He shook his head. "The people at the table laughed at me," he said. "So I ran away and hid. I think those people ate our food."

I helped Little Sam stand up. "We'll get you a new taco, okay?" I said.

"What about your burrito?" Little Sam asked.

"I'm not that hungry, anyway," I said.

After Little Sam ate his taco, we headed back to the museum. Cat and Puppy walked next to me and Little Sam. I held his hand tightly the whole time.

"Who was Teacher Todd talking to at lunch?" I asked.

"I don't know. I've never seen him before," Cat said.

"I've seen him before," said Puppy.

"You have?" I asked, surprised.

"So have I," said Little Sam. "He came to our classroom one time to visit Teacher Todd."

"Really?" Cat said.

"Yup," said Puppy.

"Do you know what his name is?" I asked.

"Mr. Kister," Little Sam said. "I always remember names. But I don't know why he talks to Teacher Todd. He's not a teacher."

"And he's not anybody's dad," said Puppy.

"Weird," I said quietly. "What's that about?"

Cat shrugged. We reached the big double doors that led to the museum. The rest of the Buddies were already inside. As we reached them they both swung open. A woman in a fancy business suit came barreling out.

"Excuse me," she said.

We jumped to the side to make room. A man in a wrinkled suit hurried after her. As he walked, his glasses kept slipping. He had to keep pushing them back up his nose.

"Please, Ms. Glick," he said. "Try to understand."

The woman stopped and spun to face him. He was so startled he nearly fell over.

"I don't want to hear any excuses, Mr. Barns!" she said. "This museum will be mine. If my mall is to expand, I need this museum space!"

"But I'm trying to tell you, Ms. Glick," the man said. "As your accountant, I cannot find the money needed to improve our offer."

Ms. Glick nearly growled.

Mr. Barns frowned. "We have some money left in charitable giving, but —"

"Bah!" Ms. Glick said. "How will that help?"

Mr. Barns shrugged. "I don't know," he said. "But it's the only money we have left to spend this year."

Finally Ms. Glick turned away and stomped off toward her mall. Mr. Barns took a deep breath and hurried after her.

"That answers that question," I said. "We know who wants the museum space."

Cat nodded. "But we still don't know who Mr. Kister is," she said.

"Or if he has anything to do with this," I said.

We didn't get to wonder about it for long. The moment we stepped into the lobby of the museum, a huge crowd, all shouting at once, stopped us.

"This museum is a mess!" shouted a mother.

"I tore my pants on a broken railing," a dad yelled. "See?" He pointed at his butt, where his polka-dotted underpants poked out of a big hole.

"And my son is covered in grease," a mom called out. "There's a leak in the Work Zone!"

"Please, please!" said Mr. Bundt. "All your complaints will be addressed!"

"It's too late!" said a dad at the back of the crowd. "We're leaving. And we're canceling our membership. This place is falling apart!"

He stormed past us, dragging his two kids by the hands, and left.

"That goes for us too!" a mom shouted. She left too. A bunch of other parents and kids followed.

Mr. Bundt hung his head and sighed. "This isn't good," he said.

He walked away, through the door to the museum offices.

"Wow," Cat said. "I guess the vandal is winning this time."

"Looks that way," I said. "I think we better talk to that accountant, Mr. Barns."

"I'm telling you," Gum said. "Connor and I have talked it over. You're over-thinking this."

"Is that right?" I asked.

"That's right," said Connor. "It's the Gutman brothers."

"You always think it's a Gutman," I said to Gum.

"You always think it's a Gutman," Little Sam said to Connor at the same time.

I patted Little Sam on the head. This kid was getting better all the time.

Gum smiled smugly. "Look at this," he said. He unzipped his backpack and pulled out a pack of apple juice boxes.

"So?" I asked.

"Apple juice," said Connor. "Skip Gutman drinks one or two of those every single day. I took these from his brother's bag."

"You stole them?" Little Sam asked.

"Well," Connor said. His face went red. "I needed the evidence. But look!" He held up the pack of juice boxes. "One is missing!"

"So?" Egg said.

"So maybe he poured it out in the baby area," Gum said. "Didn't you say there was a major apple juice incident this morning?"

"Sure," said Egg. "But we also just had lunch. Skip probably drank it then."

"That's what he wants us to believe," Gum whispered. He squinted across the room, where Anton and his little brother were working on a tower of blocks so they could knock it down as loudly as possible.

"It's pretty thin," I said, "but they are on the suspect list."

"Thank you," said Gum. "That's all we ask."

"But they're not our prime suspects," I quickly added. "Ms. Glick has to be at the top of the list." I told Egg and Gum about the mall owner and her accountant.

Egg nodded. "I think that pretty much seals it," he said.

"Just one thing remains," I said. "We have to sneak out of here and find Ms. Glick if we're going to question her."

"How are we going to do that?" Little Sam asked.

I admit I was stumped. Before I had much of a chance to think about it, though, Teacher Todd strode up.

"Hello, Buddies," he said. He waved over the Gutmans. "We're heading to the theater now. It's a special showing of *All About Aardvarks* just for the Buddies."

He led us to the museum theater. When the lights went down, our opportunity came up. A few minutes into the movie, I heard some shuffling from the back row.

Carefully, I turned in my seat. "Little Sam," I whispered. "Look." We watched Teacher Todd tiptoe from the theater.

"Let's go," I said. Little Sam nodded, and off we went.

Teacher Todd hurried down the steps and through the museum lobby.

"He's heading for the mall again," I said.

"And he's acting pretty sneaky about it," Little Sam said.

I nodded, and we followed Teacher Todd through the double doors into the mall. Then we stopped short. Teacher Todd was just a few feet inside the doors, leaning against the wall.

"Shh," I said, standing behind a column. I pulled Little Sam close to me.

Teacher Todd was talking with that man, Mr. Kister, again. I couldn't hear what they were saying, but they both seemed awfully upset.

After a few minutes, the other man stomped one foot in anger. Then he stormed off.

Teacher Todd called after him. "Tell your boss this isn't over!" Then he spun and hurried back into the museum. Little Sam and I had to hunker down even more to avoid being seen.

When Teacher Todd was gone, we stood up. "What do you think that was all about?" I said.

Little Sam shrugged. "I didn't know Teacher Todd could get that angry," he said. "Maybe he's mad about the museum being such a mess today?"

"Maybe," I said. "Whatever he's angry about, he's not happy with that man's boss."

"Nope," Little Sam agreed.

I took Little Sam by the hand. "Come on," I said. "We have to get back to the theater before the film ends."

THE VANDAL

Just as we reached the theater doors, they swung open and the Buddies poured out. Teacher Todd was the last one out. He saw me and Little Sam.

"Where have you two been?" he said.

"Oh, um . . ." I said.

Little Sam cut me off. "I had to use the potty," he said. "I mean, the bathroom."

Teacher Todd screwed up his mouth and looked at us. "You two are up to something," he said.

He looked squarely at Little Sam. "This is your second vanishing act today," Teacher Todd said.

"Vanishing act?" Little Sam asked.

The Gutmans stepped up. "He's probably the vandal," said Skip.

Teacher Todd went red in the face. "What vandal?" he stammered.

Anton laughed again. "Duh. It's what everyone has been talking about. Didn't you notice?" he asked. Anton rolled his eyes. "The dork patrol thinks it's a big mystery."

"Dork patrol?" Teacher Todd said.

"You know," Anton said. "Sam and her weird friends. They're always solving mysteries. This time they're looking for the vandal."

Skip counted off on his fingers. "Broken stuff in the Work Zone. A mess in the baby room. The Shadow Screen isn't working. . . ."

While Teacher Todd listened, his face went redder and redder.

"Come on," I said, pulling Little Sam away. We left the Gutmans alone with Teacher Todd and found our friends heading for the elevator.

"Wait up," I said. Little Sam and I got onto the elevator at the last moment, and I hit the button for the third floor.

"What's on the third floor?" Gum said.

"The Book Nook," I said, winking at Little Sam. "It's a good quiet spot, and we have to talk. On the way, I'll need to make a quick call."

CHAPTER TEN

"It all makes sense," said Cat when I was done explaining my theory.

"But we need proof," Gum said.

"That's where Mr. Barns comes in," I said. "He seems like the type who would be helpful."

"And easy to break," said Little Sam.

We all stared at him, eyes wide.

"That's something they say in detective stories sometimes," he said.

We kept staring at him.

"My mom reads them to me sometimes," Little Sam said. "She skips the scary parts."

I smiled at him. "So now we have to find him," I said. "I bet he'll squeal."

"How are we going to do that?" Cat said. She looked at her watch. "We're leaving soon."

Before I could answer, the hanging birds over our heads creaked and swung. Then they fell! The birds crashed to the lobby floor and smashed to bits as people screamed.

The Buddies ran to the railing to look down at the chaos. Standing there were Mr. Bundt, Mr. Kister, and Mr. Barns.

"Here's our chance," I said. We ran down the steps.

"What happened here, Mr. Bundt?" asked Mr. Kister.

"I — I —" said Mr. Bundt. "I just can't understand how that could have happened. Those birds have been hanging there for — well, since the museum opened!"

Mr. Barns shook his head and smiled. "I'll have the Safety Commissioner here in minutes, Mr. Bundt," he said. "It looks like you will lose the museum after all."

Mr. Bundt put his hands on his face.

I stood next to Mr. Barns. "What happened?" I asked.

"Isn't it obvious?" he said. "The museum is falling apart."

"Who is this guy?" I asked, thumbing toward the other man.

"Mr. Kister?" he said, surprised at the question. "He's Ms. Glick's assistant."

"Ms. Glick? Is that the woman who yelled at you?" Little Sam asked.

Mr. Barns fixed his glasses. He didn't answer Little Sam.

Just then, Teacher Todd came running down the stairs. "I heard a crash," he said. He hurried over to us Buddies. At the same moment, the Gutman brothers walked up too. They were both grinning, ear to ear.

"You two look awfully guilty to me," said Gum. Connor nodded.

"Oh, shush, you two," said Little Sam. "I think we all know who the culprit is here."

"Care to explain it, Little Sam?" I asked. I was sure my buddy had figured out the case.

"Happy to," he said. "As my buddy well knows, this was not vandalism for its own sake."

The grown-ups looked at Little Sam like he had two heads. I guess all that reading made him pretty well spoken.

"From the Book Nook to the falling birds, someone wanted to make the museum look bad," he said.

"Why?" he asked. "The same old reason: greed."

I leaned down close to Little Sam's ear and said, "Your mom reads you a *lot* of detective stories, doesn't she?"

He smiled and continued. "At first I thought Ms. Glick was behind this," he said, "but I don't think she knew anything about the dealings between Mr. Kister and someone very close to us Buddies."

He spun and pointed at Teacher Todd. "Our kindergarten teacher!" he said. "That is the museum vandal!"

"Me?" Teacher Todd said. He put a hand on his chest like he was shocked. "Why would I do anything like that?"

As Teacher Todd spoke, Mr. Kister started to back out of the lobby, toward to the mall exit. He didn't know the Gutmans were standing behind him. They each stuck out a foot.

"Whoa!" Mr. Kister said as he tumbled backward. He landed with a splash in the fund-raising wishing pool near the doors.

Little Sam and I ran over to the pool. I put my hands on my hips. "He's why," I said.

"Wait a minute," said Mr. Bundt. "I don't get it."

"It's simple," I said. "Mr. Kister needed the museum out of this space, so his boss could expand the mall."

"I know that part," Mr. Bundt said. "But what about Teacher Todd?"

"I think I can answer that," Ms. Glick said as she came stomping into the lobby with two big security guards.

"Ms. — Ms. Glick!" Mr. Kister said. He struggled to climb out of the pool.

"Mr. Kister knew we couldn't improve our offer to buy out the museum," she went on. "So he promised our charitable-giving fund to your kindergarten teacher."

"If he helped shut down the museum for good," Gum said. He was catching on.

I tapped my nose. "You got it, Gum," I said. "But it didn't work."

Teacher Todd tried to chuckle, like it was all nonsense. But he was also shuffling toward the door.

"Not so fast, Teacher Todd," said Little Sam. Chloe, Connor, and Puppy hurried to block the exit. Just then, Detective Jones of the River City Police Department walked in.

"There you are, Sam," he said. "I got your message. Something about a sabotage plot at the museum."

Mr. Kister was finally out of the pool and dripping all over the lobby.

"And here are your culprits," I said.

The Buddies pushed their teacher toward the detective.

"The kindergarten teacher?" the detective said.

Teacher Todd hung his head. "The school needs money," he said.

"So does this museum," said Mr. Bundt. He was furious. "What you two have done here could have shut down the museum for good."

"This is not how I want to do business, Mr. Kister," said Ms. Glick. "You're fired."

Detective Jones cuffed both men and led them out of the museum.

"You kids did a great thing today," Mr. Bundt said. "If the museum had lost all its members for good, we never would have had the funding to stay open — here or anywhere."

"This isn't how I want to acquire this space, Mr. Bundt," said Ms. Glick.

Mr. Bundt nodded. "And we can't afford to move," he said. "There's a great space I've had my eye on in the warehouse district, but it's not affordable."

Ms. Glick suddenly grinned. "Perhaps if you got a large donation," she said. "Maybe then you could afford to move?"

Mr. Bundt beamed. "We sure could," he said. "That's exactly what we need."

Mr. Barns pulled out his smartphone and poked the screen.

"I think we just found a great recipient for that charitable-giving fund," he said.

Someone grabbed my hand. I looked down. There was Little Sam. "We saved the children's museum," he said.

"Yup," I said.

"There's still one question, though," said Gum. We stepped outside and stood on the sidewalk in front of the museum.

"What's that?" I asked, glancing at Gum.

"How are we going to get back to school?" he asked. "Teacher Todd drove the van!"

literary news

MYSTERIOUS WRITER REVEALED!

Steve Brezenoff lives in Minneapolis, Minnesota, with his wife, Beth, and their son, Sam. Besides writing books, he enjoys playing video games, riding his bicycle, and helping middle-school students work on their writing skills. Steve's ideas almost always come to him in his dreams, so he does his best writing in his pajamas.

arts & entertainment

ARTIST IS KEY TO SOLVING MYSTERY, SAY POLICE

Marcos Calo lives happily in A Coruña, Spain, with his wife, Patricia (who is also an illustrator), and their daughter, Claudia. When Marcos and Patricia aren't drawing, they like to go on long walks by the sea. They also watch a lot of films and eat Nutella sandwiches. Yum!

A Detective's Dictionary

charitable (CHAR-i-tuh-buhl)—related to giving money to people in need

culprit (KUHL-prit)—a person who is guilty of doing something wrong or of committing a crime

evidence (EV-uh-duhnss)—facts that help prove something or make you believe that something is true

frantically (FRAN-tik-lee)—in a wild, fearful way

investigator (in-VESS-tuh-gay-tor)—a person who tries to find out as much as possible to solve a crime

nonsense (NON-senss)—something that has no meaning

obvious (OB-vee-uhss)—easy to see or understand

recipient (ri-SIP-ee-uhnt)—a person who receives something

sabotage (SAB-uh-tahzh)—the deliberate damage or destruction of property

suspects (SUH-spekts)—people thought to have committed a crime

theory (THEE-ur-ee)—an idea that explains how something happened

vandal (VAN-duhl)—someone who needlessly damages or destroys other people's property

Sam Archer

Kindergarten Buddies

(A)

Children's Museums

I admit it. I was not looking forward to this trip to the children's museum. But after I researched these museums, I decided that they were more interesting than I thought.

The Brooklyn Children's Museum, the first children's museum in the world, was started in 1899. The founders wanted the museum to be a place just for children.

At first, the museum's main focus was teaching city kids about nature. As time went on, exhibits on technology and culture were added.

Throughout the next century, hundreds of children's museums were built in the United States. But it wasn't until 1978 that Europe get their first children's museum. Le Musee des Enfants in Brussels, Belgium, was inspired by the Boston Children's Museum.

The museum I would most like to visit is the world's biggest. The Children's Museum of Indianapolis is nearly 473,000 square feet. The outside has giant dinosaur models that look like they are breaking into or out of the museum. Inside there are 120,000 artifacts--all kid-friendly.

Sam, I am sorry that Teacher Todd behaved badly on the field trip. Thank you for your fine detective work.

-Mr. S

FURTHER INVESTIGATIONS

CASE #FTM2OSAKBCM

1. Sam joined Kindergarten Buddies just because her grandparents and friends wanted her to. Have you ever done something only because other people asked you to? Talk about it.

2. Was Sam a good Kindergarten Buddy? Explain your answer.

3. At the end, the students had to figure out a way to get back to the school. What do you think they did?

IN YOUR OWN DETECTIVE'S NOTEBOOK . . .

1. Everyone's Kindergarten Buddy shared similar personalities. If you had a Kindergarten Buddy, what would he or she be like?

2. Have you ever been to a children's museum? Pretend you are trying to convince someone to go to the same museum, and describe one of the best exhibits there.

3. Imagine that Ms. Glick was actually the museum vandal. Write a new ending where Sam and Little Sam confront her.

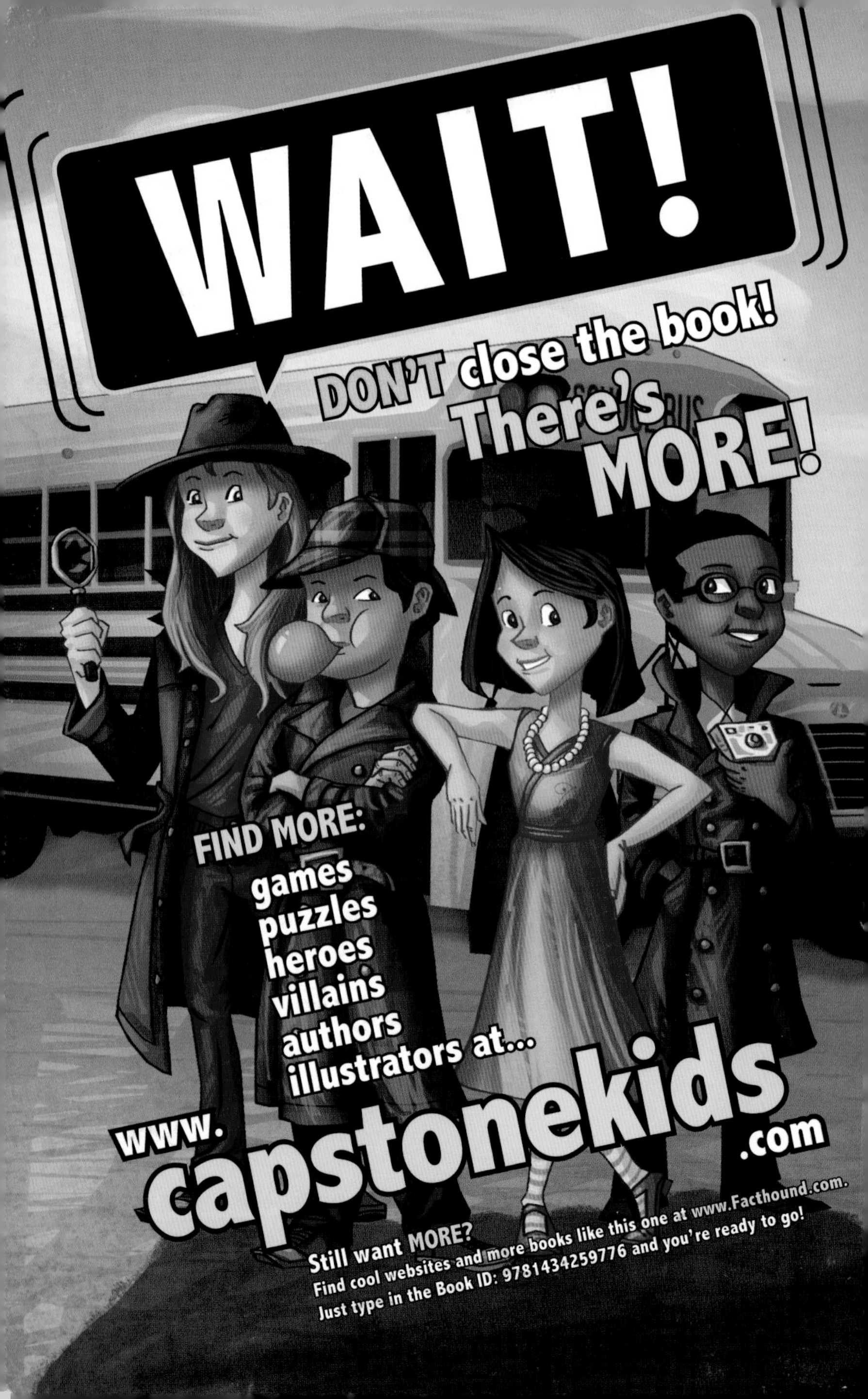
WAIT!
DON'T close the book!
There's MORE!
FIND MORE:
games
puzzles
heroes
villains
authors
illustrators at...
www.capstonekids.com
Still want MORE?
Find cool websites and more books like this one at www.Facthound.com.
Just type in the Book ID: 9781434259776 and you're ready to go!